# MOST WANTED

# MOST WANTED

# -Kate Thompson-

Illustrated by Jonny Duddle

 GREENWILLOW BOOKS
*An Imprint of HarperCollinsPublishers*

Most Wanted
Copyright © 2010 by Kate Thompson
Illustrations © 2010 by Jonny Duddle

First published in 2010 in Great Britain by The Bodley Head,
an imprint of Random House Children's Books.
First published in 2010 in the United States by Greenwillow Books.

The right of Kate Thompson to be identified as the author of this work has been asserted by her.

www.harpercollinschildrens.com

The text of this book is set in Bembo.

Library of Congress Cataloging-in-Publication Data

Thompson, Kate, (date).
Highway robbery / by Kate Thompson.
p. cm.
"Greenwillow Books."
Summary: In first century Rome, in the turmoil after a rumor circulates that mad Emperor "Little Boots" is dead, young Marcus brings home a horse that the emperor had proclaimed a consul and his family decides they must treat it as an honored guest.
ISBN 978-0-06-173037-5 (trade bdg.)
[1. Horses—Fiction. 2. Family life—Rome—Fiction. 3. Bakers—Fiction. 4. Caligula, Emperor of Rome, 12-41—Fiction. 5. Rome—History—Caligula, 37-41—Fiction.]
I. Title.   PZ7.T3715965Mos 2010   [Fic]—dc22   2009034952

10  11  12  13  14  CG/RRDB  First Edition 10 9 8 7 6 5 4 3 2 1

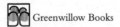 Greenwillow Books

For my big brothers,
Ben and Mark

# MOST
# WANTED

# CHAPTER ONE

It was early afternoon on a cold February day. I had just finished my deliveries and was making my way home across the city with my handcart. The streets were quiet, as they usually were at that time of day, so I had no trouble hearing the horse when it came trotting up behind me, and I moved aside with my cart to let it pass.

But it didn't. The young man who was leading it stopped beside me, and when I turned to look at him, I was astonished by what I saw.

He was a slave, and I might have been struck by how well dressed he was if I hadn't noticed that the horse was dressed even better. It wore a blanket of royal purple and its head collar was decorated with precious stones that sparkled in rainbow colors. Its lead rope was a chain of solid gold. I stood with my mouth open, astonished. I ought to have known immediately what horse this was, for everyone in the city knew about Incitatus, but sometimes my mind

doesn't work very quickly, especially when it comes up against the impossible.

"There is a rumor going around," the slave boy said. "Terrible news."

He was panting hard and gasping out the words, and he had a strong English accent as well, so it wasn't easy for me to understand what he was saying.

"News?" I said.

"But it can't be true," he said. "I have to go and find out."

"Find out what?" I said.

"Here," he said, thrusting the golden chain into my hand. "Take care of him. I'll find out the truth and come straight back."

And before I could object, he was

gone, running down the street the way he had come. The nerve of him! A slave telling me what to do! I couldn't hold his horse for him, no matter how smartly it was dressed. I called out after him, but if he heard me, he paid no attention. At the end of the street he hesitated and looked up and down. Then he slipped around the corner and was gone.

My brother needed the handcart to collect flour from the mill, and I had to get home. If I was late, I would be in serious trouble. I had been out on my round since before dawn, and I needed to get something to eat and go to bed for a few hours because my whole family had to work through the night to have fresh bread ready for the morning. On a good day I got about five hours' sleep in the evening. On a good day my mother and father got three.

It hadn't always been like that. Life was a whole lot easier for all of us before the emperor, Gaius, took our horses and the best of our slaves. They say he sold the slaves and used the horses to transport Rome's treasures to Gaul, so he could sell them, because he never had enough money for all his mad and extravagant projects.

I don't know if it's true, and I don't really care. The end result was the same for us. Our lives became a long, hard, circular grind of baking and loading and delivering and sleeping and getting up and baking again. And I didn't have time to be standing around holding horses, no matter how glamorous they were.

And he really was glamorous. A racing horse, I was sure, from the look of his light bones and his fine, shiny coat. He tossed his head and looked around him with wild, fiery eyes, and he sniffed warily at my empty cart as though he expected it to jump up and bite him.

You'd have guessed by now, I'm sure, because everyone—even people from out of town like yourself—had heard about Emperor Gaius and the things his madness caused him to do, but I still hadn't worked out whose horse it was that I was taking care of.

While I was trying to decide what to do, a man came along the street: a wealthy man, from the shape of his belly and the cut of his toga. He stopped in front of the horse and, to my amazement, gave a bow.

"How nice to see you out and about, Consul Incitatus," he said. "Taking a little exercise, are you? Getting to know your citizens?"

My knees went so weak that they would barely support me. This was absurd, it had to be a nightmare. It couldn't be happening.

"And you must be the consul's companion," said the man, looking me up and down and making a clear effort to disguise his surprise and contempt. I'm a baker, after all. We have a tendency to be more than a little dusty.

I was rooted to the spot, my mind in turmoil. You see, the horse I was holding was a lot more than just a horse.

After the emperor the two consuls
are Rome's most powerful officials, as
I'm sure you know. If I were holding
a dragon, it couldn't have been more
dangerous.

"Yes, sir," I stammered. "His companion. Indeed. For today, that is."

Our consuls are elected by the people,
but this one was an exception. Emperor
Gaius had flouted the senate and made
the decision himself. I found myself
stroking the horse's neck, realized that
this was no way to behave toward a
consul, and stood to a kind of trem-
bling attention. The rich man's eyes
darkened.

"That is," I spluttered, "the consul is

taking a stroll and I am accompanying him."

I could tell that the man didn't believe a word I said, but what could he do? I saw a slim possibility of escape and leaped at it.

"Perhaps you would care to accompany him back to the palace yourself, sir?" I said, offering him the golden chain.

He backed away as though he had just noticed that I was a leper and simpered something about very urgent business. He bowed again to the horse, reversed a few steps in that position, then turned and scuttled away down the street as fast as his plump legs would carry him.

# CHAPTER TWO

Under other circumstances I might have found it funny to see that man's undignified retreat. But I was in far too much danger to laugh. If I was caught, I was done for.

You might think that appointing a horse as your second-in-command was a clever kind of joke, but I can assure you there was nothing funny about Emperor Gaius and his madness. We had all celebrated when he took over as our emperor. Anything had to be better than Tiberius. That's what we thought, anyway. It just goes to show how wrong you can be.

Little Boots, we called him, because he used to wear miniature versions of soldiers' boots when he was a child. Sounds so innocent and affectionate, doesn't it? And it was to begin with. But by the time that golden chain was put into my hand, the mention of the name was enough to make my blood run cold. He had become a monster, a tyrant of the worst imaginable kind.

I had to get out of there, and as soon as I could persuade my legs to move, I tried to make a run for it. I dropped the chain, picked up the handles of my cart, and set out for home.

But the consul Incitatus had other ideas. He had his own house next to the palace, where important people went to have dinner with him, and a retinue of servants who looked after him night and day. He wasn't used to being alone. So when I went off down the street, he followed me, dragging the end of his golden chain along the cobbles.

Alarmed as I was, I couldn't bring myself to shout and wave my arms at one of Rome's consuls, so there wasn't much I could do to stop him. I put down the handles of the handcart again, and I was still trying to work out what to do when I heard running footsteps and turned to see a boy of about my own age racing up behind me. There was something about his urgency that made me realize he wasn't on any ordinary errand, and I remembered what the slave had said about "terrible news."

"What's going on?" I called to the boy.

He glanced at me as he raced past, but he didn't reply.

I looked back the way he had come. There was activity at the crossroads back there. I could see soldiers heading toward the palace and a flurry of people moving rapidly in the opposite direction. My innards began to churn in panic. I knew the city well, and I could read the signs. Something big was happening. And if Little Boots was behind it, as he was behind everything that happened in

Rome, it meant that no one was safe.

My instinct was to bolt, but if I returned to the bakery without the cart, I was going to find myself in a different kind of trouble. So I grabbed the handles again and started trundling the stupid, clumsy thing along the street.

And still the consul Incitatus followed me.

There was a shout from behind. I turned and saw the English slave who had left me holding the horse. He was running down the street toward me, but my initial sense of relief didn't last longer than a heartbeat. He was being pursued by a soldier, and the soldier was winning.

"Save him!" the boy yelled at me, and they were the last words he ever said, because at that moment the soldier caught him and ran him through with his sword.

There were other soldiers in the street and they had seen me. It was impossible to miss me, in fact, with the horse's big purple blanket blazing out like a flag. There was only one way now for me to save my life, and I have to admit that I didn't stop to think about the consequences. They could be no worse than staying where I was. So I jumped from the ground to the handcart and from the handcart onto Incitatus's purple-coated back, and I dug my heels into the consul's sides as hard as I possibly could.

# CHAPTER THREE

Everything had been fine at first. Little Boots did some great things for Rome when he first came to power. But then he became ill.

I was young at the time, but I still remember it well. My parents and grandparents paced the floor with worry. They joined the crowds at the temples, spending huge sums of money on sacrifices to the gods, pleading with them to spare the life of our young Caesar.

Be careful what you ask of the gods, because they might grant your wishes. In this case they did, and many's the person who has lived to regret the prayers and sacrifices he or she made at that time.

Little Boots survived his illness, but

most people will tell you that he never recovered from it. It changed him entirely. He began to say that he was a god, and he had the heads removed from all the statues of Zeus and replaced with his own likeness.

He spent all the money that was left in the treasury on crazy things like floating palaces, and then he came up with ways to take everyone else's money so he could keep on indulging himself.

My grandfather was one of his first victims. He was a respected figure in

Rome, and our bakery was the biggest and the best. So when Little Boots closed the granaries one day and wouldn't let out any grain for making bread, my grandfather went to see him to ask why. It wasn't only our business that would suffer. Without bread the people of Rome would be hungry.

Later that day my father and mother received an invitation to go to the palace for dinner. They always refused to tell me what happened, but my brother, Lucius, found out and he told me. My parents were made to watch my grandfather being executed, and afterward they had to sit and have dinner with Little Boots and pretend to make small talk and laugh at his jokes. And they had, because if they hadn't there was a good chance that their heads would have rolled like my grandfather's, and what would have become of us children then?

If there is one thing to be thankful for, it is that my grandfather's death was relatively quick and painless. Since those days Little Boots has become ingenious at finding new ways to kill people. The longer it takes and the more painful it is, the better he likes it. And that's why when I got up on that horse's back, it wasn't for a lark. I was more frightened than I had ever been before. I was relying on the consul Incitatus to save my life.

# CHAPTER FOUR

When I was small, before Little Boots took our cart horses, I was sometimes allowed to sit up on one of them while our good old slave Drusus led it on the delivery round. I never got to go faster than a shambling kind of trot, but I did at least know how it felt to have a horse underneath me.

If I hadn't, I'm sure Incitatus would have lost me in the first three strides. He took off as though he were back on the racecourse, as if he were sick and tired of being a consul and wanted nothing more than a good gallop around the streets.

I clung to his thick mane and prayed to Artemis to keep me safe. The purple blanket was no substitute for a saddle, but it could have been worse. In the summertime, so I'd heard, Incitatus wore a silk one, and if he had been wearing that now, my head would have been bouncing off the cobbles.

I couldn't remember how to steer. I'm not sure I ever learned, because the cart horses always had someone leading them. I wanted to turn to the right, but the end of the chain was in my left hand and on the left side of the horse's neck. But if I pulled it and turned left, it would lead me back toward the center of the city, straight into the swords of the palace guard.

The desire to stay alive gave me the courage to do something that seemed, to my inexperienced mind, to be practically impossible. I leaned forward as far as I could and passed the chain beneath the horse's neck, from my left hand to my right. Just in the nick of time I pulled on it. The consul's head turned, and we skidded around the corner and into the next street.

Sparks flew from his shoes. Seeing the open stretch of the street ahead of him,

Incitatus dropped his head and increased his speed. He swerved around a porter carrying a huge sack, who must have been deaf because he didn't get out of the way. Everyone else in that street squeezed themselves flat against the walls as we went thundering by, the purple blanket fluttering like an empty sail behind us.

I changed hands again and turned Incitatus sharply to the left, into an alley that was too narrow for a cart. A girl flattened herself into a doorway. I saw the breeze of our passage ruffle her hair as we shot past. A smaller child squealed and called for his mother and crouched beneath the open window of his house in terror.

Left again, not so sharply this time, and into another narrow street with tall apartment buildings leaning in to meet one another above our heads and shutting out the light. They were badly built, most of those places, and several of them had collapsed over the past few years. Dozens of people had been killed, but there was no help for the survivors. Not from the builders or from the landlords or from the emperor. They could sleep on the streets for all anyone cared, and the truth is a lot of them did.

To the right again now, and then left, and straight on across another main thoroughfare. I prayed that it wouldn't be filled with soldiers looking for Incitatus. It wasn't, but just as we got there our crossing was blocked by two more of our bakery handcarts, both of them empty. One was being pushed by my brother Lucius, the other by my cousin Quintus. They heard the horse charging toward them and abandoned the carts. Incitatus hesitated, but he was going far too fast

to stop. He altered his stride, and I felt
the decision through his body as he pow-
ered forward and gathered himself for the
jump. I clung on, certain of disaster, but
the consul cleared the carts with ease and
plunged straight on into the opposite
street.

One more
right turn, then
one more, and
I was home.
At the gates
of our yard I
hauled on the
golden chain.
The horse was
reluctant to stop,

and we overshot the gates and went on several more yards before I got him under control and turned him back. I slid off and leaned, weak-kneed and quivering, against our compound gates.

# CHAPTER FIVE

I have a bit of a reputation in my family and it's not really fair. Whenever anything goes missing or gets broken, I'm blamed for it, whether it's my fault or not. It's true that I'm a bit on the clumsy side and my arms and legs don't always go exactly where I want them to, but it's still not right to blame everything on me.

I did lose two sacks of wheat once, but that was because a lad tricked me into going to look at an enormous fish, and while I was gone, some other lads robbed my cart. And it's true that I once harnessed the wrong ox to the grinder. It was a young one that hadn't been properly trained, and it went berserk and pulled the whole thing to pieces. But everyone makes

mistakes sometimes,

don't they?

I'm not really a walking disaster, but I have to admit I found myself wondering about it as I hammered on the compound gates. Maybe it would have been smarter to keep riding until I reached the outskirts of the city and then abandon the horse when he was too tired to follow me home. But you know what? I couldn't have done it.

I was flushed with excitement after the race through town, and I was totally besotted with the horse that had shared the adventure with me. He had looked after me, done what I asked, and brought me safely home. He had outrun the soldiers, kept his feet on the uneven stones of the streets, and jumped a pair of handcarts. I wouldn't have abandoned him now if Little Boots himself had arrived to collect him.

Well. Maybe I would.

"Who is it?" my father called through the gates.

"It's me, Marcus," I said. "And . . . and I've brought the consul Incitatus home with me."

# CHAPTER SIX

Incitatus and I stood in the middle of the yard as the crowd around us grew. First there was only my father, staring at us as if we had dropped out of the clouds, and then he was joined by my two sisters, Tiberia and Appia, and my mother, and then my aunt came out of her house with two more of my cousins, and then my grandmother and the two elderly slaves who still looked after her.

None of them wanted to believe that

the horse was the consul Incitatus. My father wanted to strip all the finery off him and turn him out into the lane.

"Whatever he is, he's trouble," he said. "How could you be so stupid as to bring him here?"

I told the story again, carefully explaining that I'd had no choice, but no one seemed to understand.

"Better to keep the horse and throw the boy out," said my aunt. "He's nothing but trouble and always has been."

I saw my mother turn on her and braced myself for another of their interminable arguments, but just then Incitatus raised his tail and dropped a heap of steaming manure onto the dusty floor

of the yard. That
silenced everyone.
Not because of
the smell and the

mess. We have always had animals in the yard—horses in the old days, only oxen now. It was what we saw in the dung that left us all speechless. It glittered. It shone. It was full of tiny sparkling pieces of gold.

That was another of the stories that everyone had heard about the emperor's favorite horse but no one ever quite believed: Incitatus was fed on mangoes and apples and on oats mixed through with gold flakes.

My aunt looked around. With the gates closed no one could see into our compound, but all the same it was as though there were eyes everywhere. We all felt it. My older sister, Appia, scooped the dung into a bucket and hid it underneath the lemon tree.

"We have to get him out of sight," my mother said. She opened the door to

one of the stables and let our three dogs
out. Two of the other stables had broken
roofs, and the remaining ones had gradu-
ally filled with junk since the horses had
gone.

I led Incitatus to the door. He stopped.

"Come on," I said. "Nice stable for you,
see?"

But the consul did not agree and refused
to go in. My father raised his arms and
growled at him, but Incitatus laid back
his ears and ignored him.

"Get him in!" said my aunt, and we
could all hear the panic in her voice.
"Quickly! Before someone comes and
sees him."

Appia fetched the whip we use to drive

the oxen on the grinder. My father raised it threateningly, but Incitatus took exception to this and reversed determinedly away from the stable door, dragging me helplessly with him.

"Stupid boy!" said my aunt, but neither she nor my father dared actually use the whip on Incitatus. Horse or no horse, he was one of Rome's consuls and a member of the emperor's household.

"At least take off the purple robe," said my mother.

But no one dared to do that, either, and while we were all standing around wondering what to do next, there was a loud knock at the yard gates.

The dogs barked. Everyone froze where

they stood, with the exception of Incitatus, who gave me a hard nudge with his nose and began to walk over to the inviting double doors of the bakery. I pulled him up, but my mother shook her head and gestured to me to take him in there.

This time he didn't hesitate but marched straight into the dark, sweet-scented building. I can't say I blamed him. It was a palace compared with that small, doggy stable. My mother closed the door behind us, and I heard my father quiet the dogs and ask who was at the gates.

"Quintus and Lucius," came my brother's voice. "Let us in, quick!"

Even behind the bakery doors I could hear the monstrous sigh as everyone let out their breaths together. The gates creaked, and the handcarts rattled in. I knocked. My mother opened the doors a crack and let me out.

"Have you heard the news?" Lucius was saying.

"What news?" said my father.

But my brother waited until the gates were firmly closed and bolted and the family gathered in a close huddle around him before he would say any more. Even then he whispered as he told us what he had heard.

"It isn't certain," he said, "but they're saying on the street that Little Boots is dead."

# CHAPTER SEVEN

**Y**ou would expect us to celebrate, perhaps, to clap and cheer and dance around the compound with delight. We didn't. Instead a silence fell over us, so profound that even the dogs stopped their energetic activities and slumped down in the dust.

Behind the bakery doors Incitatus whickered anxiously, and I heard the *thud-thud-thud* of more of his golden droppings landing on the spotless floor.

Every one of us hoped that what we had heard was true, but every one of us, from my aged grandmother right down to my seven-year-old cousin, was thinking the same thing.

It was a trick.

It would be just like Little Boots to do something like that: spread the word that he was dead and then, while people are celebrating and sacrificing victims to the gods, send out his soldiers to arrest them all for disloyalty. Then he could confiscate their property and use the proceeds to finance his perverted pleasures, and send them to the Circus Maximus to fight his professional gladiators, or cut off their hands and string them around their

necks, or feed them to his lions and alli-
gators and other dreadful beasts.

But we would not fall into that trap.
We stayed silent. Incitatus whickered
again, and I opened one of the doors so
he could see us.

"We continue as usual," said my grandmother at last. She spoke softly, afraid of
eavesdroppers. "We do nothing and say

nothing until we smell the smoke from his funeral pyre."

"Not even then," said my father. "I would need more proof than that."

"Who will be emperor next?" said my little sister, Tiberia.

"Shhh," said my mother. "Hold your tongue."

We had a plan then, about how to react to the rumor. But we still had a serious problem on our hands.

"What are we going to do about the consul?" I said.

"The best plan," said my father, "is to wait until dark, then strip all the finery off him and turn him loose in the street."

"That kind of plan never works," said my mother. "There's always some child or a nosy old sweeper who's bound to see you. And what would it look like, turning loose a perfectly good horse?"

My grandmother agreed. "The emperor would have us in our own ovens if he ever found out we did that."

"In any case," I said, "Incitatus likes us. If we turn him out, he won't go any-where. He'll just stand outside the gates until we let him back in."

My aunt glared at me, but she didn't say anything.

"So there are two choices, as far as I can see," said my mother. "We take him back to the palace and hand him over, or we keep him here, hidden away until we discover what has happened."

"There's another thing we can do," said my tough cousin Quintus. "We can cut him up and feed him to the dogs."

Lucius grinned. "That would serve Little Boots right."

My grandmother stepped forward into our midst. "Now listen, all of you," she said. "That boy"—she poked me hard in the collarbone—"came riding in here this afternoon at a very high speed. The horse is wearing a purple robe and a head collar dripping with jewels. Does everyone here really believe that no one will have noticed?"

Everyone didn't. When we stopped to

think about it, *no* one did.

"Someone somewhere knows that Incitatus is here," my grandmother went on. "So losing him or feeding him to the dogs will do us no good."

Quintus shrugged, but everyone else nodded, and my grandmother continued. "It's my opinion that your son, my own grandson, signed a death sentence for everyone in this family when he brought Incitatus to these gates."

My heart stopped and my breath got stuck in my throat. I felt as though I were already standing in front of Little Boots, waiting to hear what particular horrors he had chosen for me.

"No!" I managed to blurt.

"He didn't mean it," said my mother, moving closer to me.

"Always the same," said my grand- mother. "Never stops to think."

"Well, what would you have done in his position?" asked my mother indignantly.

"What I would have done is beside the point," said my grandmother. "It's what we do now that will decide whether we live or die."

"And that is . . . ?" said my father.

"We treat the consul as an honored guest. You invite him into your house and give him the best bedroom."

"*My* house!" said my father. "Why not your house?"

"Because mine is humble and small and yours is large and elegant. Or at least it used to be when I lived in it."

He had to concede the point. "And what then?" he said. "What happens if they discover him here?"

"Then we tell the truth. We say that we heard dreadful rumors concerning the health of the emperor, and your son witnessed unrest and violence not far from the palace. For the consul's own safety he invited him to reside with us until the situation settled down and the true facts became known."

"I invited him?" I said.

"Indeed you did," said my grandmother. "And he most graciously accepted."

# CHAPTER EIGHT

I didn't sleep much that night. I doubt whether anyone in our compound did, but I know I slept least of all.

We had tried to leave the consul Incitatus alone, once we had covered the floor of our guest bedroom with fresh straw and given him as much hay and oats as our bullocks would eat in a week. But he wasn't used to being on his own, and he wouldn't settle. Needless to say, I was the one who was sent in to keep him company.

I was very comfortable, actually. The bed in that room had been built in there and wouldn't fit out of the door, so we had pushed it against the wall to make room for the horse. I unrolled my own mattress on it, and I was as comfortable as I would have been anywhere.

So it wasn't discomfort that kept me awake. It was fear. Fear that Incitatus would be discovered and that Little Boots wouldn't accept our excuses. My head filled with florid imaginings, and I dredged up all the memories I had of the ways Little Boots had invented for putting people to death. They went from bad to worse to unthinkable. I wondered whether anyone had ever been given a choice and which method I would pick if I had to.

But I did finally get to sleep, and it was Incitatus himself who helped me.

He came close to the bedside and lay down there on the floor, and the regular swell of his breathing began to lull me. I had to admit that he was nice company, the consul, and I couldn't imagine any other member of the Roman senate being so quiet and gentle.

"Perhaps you'll be the next Caesar," I whispered into his ear.

And, imagining that, I finally slipped into sleep.

# CHAPTER NINE

For the first time in as long as I can remember, my mother didn't get me up in the middle of the night to help with the bread making. I woke to the sounds of the handcarts in the yard and the creak of the compound gates as they opened.

Incitatus was already up and nosing around in the marble basin where we'd put his oats the day before. There were fresh droppings in the straw, but you had to look very hard to see any gold in them now, because most of it had already passed through his system.

I got up and fetched him more oats, then drew water and filled up his trough. He made a big show of splashing at the water with his nose before he drank it, and I wondered whether he was used to having it warmed for him or whether we were insulting him and ought to be giving him wine instead. But he blew sweet breath into my face and stood quite

contentedly as I
groomed his mane
with my mother's
comb and pol-
ished his coat with
her best silk shawl.

I liked it very much,
this job. It was better
than delivering bread
any day.

My mother brought
me breakfast and some
fruit for Incitatus, and

afterward, because there was nothing left
to do, I climbed back into bed and went
to sleep again. I dreamed that I was riding into battle alongside Little Boots's

father, the mighty Germanicus, but I got
left behind because my horse was lame.
When I looked down, I saw its hind
legs were missing, and Little Boots was
crouching beside me, roasting them over
an open fire.

That afternoon when everyone had
returned from the deliveries, we had
another family gathering in the yard.

The streets were full of rumors and speculation, and it was impossible to know what was true.

Lucius had heard that Little Boots had been murdered by members of the prae-torian guard and that they killed his wife and baby daughter as well, but since the praetorian guard existed to look after the emperor's personal safety, it seemed impossible to us.

Other people were saying that the whole thing was a trick, as we had feared, and that there were public executions taking place beside the palace and that the streets were running with blood. This couldn't be confirmed because no one had the courage to go anywhere near there, and the streets surrounding the palace were unusually quiet and empty.

My father had heard that Little Boots's body had been taken to a private garden and they had tried to cremate it, but there hadn't been enough wood for a proper pyre and they'd had to bury what was left of him.

And someone else told my cousin that rioters had overrun the forum and that there was no longer any kind of government in the city.

But the maddest rumor of all, the one that cheered us all up and gave us a good laugh, was that there were plans afoot to crown Claudius as the next

Caesar. He was Little Boots's uncle and the only member of his family who had escaped death or banishment. It was said, and it was probably true, that Little Boots spared his life only because he enjoyed making fun of him in public. People liked him on the whole, poor, daft, stammering old Claudius, but the idea of his becoming emperor was ridiculous.

So we decided, at our gathering, to believe the worst and ignore the best and, for the meantime at least, to carry on as we were and to stick to the agreed story. The consul Incitatus was our honored guest, and we were caring for him until Rome settled down.

But that night, well after dark, a neighbor called at our gates, and she had new information. She had heard that soldiers were going from door to door throughout the city and were searching all the outbuildings. Several horses had been confiscated and their owners dragged off along with them. No one could say why. Our neighbor was aware, she said, that we had no horses now, but there was no harm in passing on the news all the same.

She did know, of course. As my grandmother had said, it would have been impossible for me to come galloping into our little back lane without someone in the neighborhood noticing. But she had been a loyal friend by tipping us off, and in dangerous times like ours there aren't so many of them left. We were lucky. Very lucky indeed.

# CHAPTER TEN

It was my little sister, Tiberia, who ran into the guest room to tell me what the neighbor had said about the soldiers and the searches. Before I could get my head around it, Lucius stormed in with the rest of the family at his heels.

"We have to get him out of here," he said. "And quickly, before the soldiers arrive and drag us all off to our deaths."

He pushed me aside and began to yank

at the buckle at
the front of
the purple
blanket.
The consul
took excep-
tion to this
and laid his ears
back and began
to back up across the room,
but it was my grandmother who
stopped my brother from going any
further.

"No," she said, and her voice carried
all the authority of her seventy years. "I
will not allow anything to be done in a
state of panic. You may be right, Lucius,

but we have to think this through and reach a proper decision."

. Lucius was red in the face with rage, but my grandmother's word was law and he didn't dare act against her. I thought I was in the clear, but now the full force of her authority was turned upon me.

"You, boy!" she said. "You will clean up this mess and put fresh straw down. Then you will polish that . . . that consul until every hair of his coat shines like gold. If they find Incitatus in here, they must have no complaints about the way he has been looked after."

I ran to get a basket to collect the dung.

When I came back,
the rest of the
family was
moving off
toward the
front of the
house to
continue their
discussions. For the moment at least, the
bread making was forgotten.

I gathered the droppings and the wet
straw and went to get some fresh stuff.
The compound was unusually quiet,
with everyone at the meeting inside
my parents' house, and as I was carrying the straw across it, I suddenly knew
that it was up to me to sort out this

problem, and that I would have to do it alone. And I knew exactly how I would have to do it.

You might think it was brave of me, but it wasn't really. Not when you stop to think about it. The way we saw it, Little Boots had sent out his soldiers to find his favorite horse—his best friend and trusted consul. Already people were being arrested because he was missing, and *they* didn't even have Incitatus. We did.

Of course, it was possible that the emperor and his soldiers would be delighted that we had invited the consul into our home and taken such care of him. Little Boots might give us back our horses and shower honors upon the whole family.

But despite what my grandmother said, I just couldn't see it happening. As I crossed the yard, I had a vision of it running with blood and littered with teeth and fingers and ears. "Put him to death so he knows he is dying"—that was one of Little Boots's milder declarations. He insisted on his victims suffering for as long as possible. Some of them took days to die. There were stories I had heard that were too dreadful to think about.

So, the question I was left with was a simple one: all of us or just one? And the answer to that was obvious: just one.

But which one?

Simple again. The one who'd caused the problem in the first place.

# CHAPTER ELEVEN

They were all talking so quietly that I couldn't hear a thing when I went into the house. The consul was pleased to see me back, and his ears pricked with excitement when I gathered up the golden chain and attached it to his head collar. As I opened the guest room door, a sudden image flashed into my mind of the statue of Jupiter in the Capitol, his head replaced by that of Little Boots,

his thunderbolt raised, ready to strike. The vision stopped me in my tracks and made my innards churn, but it didn't shake my resolve.

I took a deep breath and led Incitatus through the yard, and out of the compound gates.

There was practically no one about, and those there were kept a low profile: hooded ghosts vanishing into black corners. What I did see, though, was horses. In practically every street there was a cob or a cart horse or a child's riding pony, each of them turned out from its warm stable to save its owner from arrest. And the saddest thing of all was that not one of those beasts could possibly have been mistaken for Incitatus. It was yet another example of the terror that Little Boots created with every order he gave.

I had no clear idea of what I was doing, beyond getting Incitatus as far from my family compound as possible before I abandoned him. When I

think of it now, I see that I ought to
have stripped him of his finery before I
left home and put the blanket and the
bejeweled head collar under one of the
bread ovens to burn. I ought to have let
go of him sooner, and chased him away
down one of those dark streets and run
off before he could find me and follow

me. But a strange thing began to happen, and I became fascinated by it, and it took my attention from where it ought to have been.

The abandoned horses began to follow us. First one, then another, and then a couple more that had already joined up together. Then, with the help of a street pump, I managed to clamber up onto his back. If Incitatus minded, he didn't show it. He walked with long graceful strides, his head high, gazing around at the dim streets of Rome as though he knew that he was second-in-command only to the emperor and that the place as good as belonged to him.

And still I stayed onboard, taken in by the consul's confidence, seduced by the little procession of horses into a dream of power. When I look back on it now, I see that I wasn't in my right mind that night. I was puffed up with pride at my own heroism and filled with sweet anguish by my noble gesture of self-sacrifice. I became Germanicus, Rome's greatest hero, returning triumphant from my latest campaign. More horses joined us, my army following along behind. The rejoicing crowds parted before us. I never fathered that monster Little Boots, but I became emperor myself instead, and I was the kindest, most generous Caesar the empire had ever known.

And then, too suddenly, real soldiers were there: about eight of them and all asleep at the side of the street. I hauled on the chain, but there was no stopping Incitatus now. He shook his head and jerked on the rein and just kept going. The sounds of all those horses woke the soldiers, and they jumped up in confusion, shouting orders to each other.

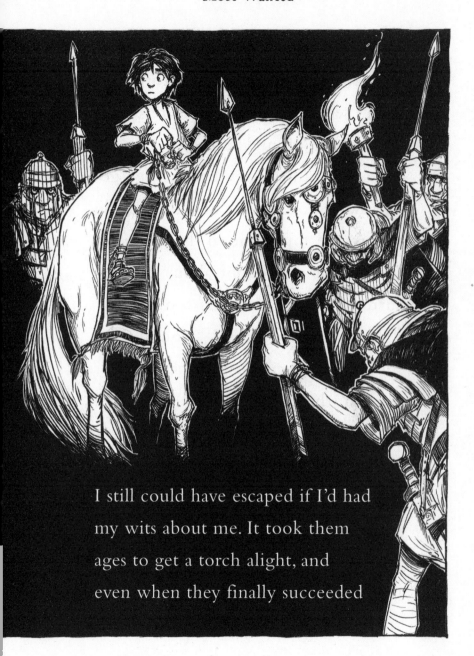

I still could have escaped if I'd had
my wits about me. It took them
ages to get a torch alight, and
even when they finally succeeded

and saw Incitatus in his fine attire, they didn't seem to know how to react. If I had slipped off and scarpered I would have been miles away before they got themselves organized, and they could never have found me in the dark. But by the time I thought about it, I was surrounded and it was far too late.

The soldiers stood around and looked at the consul, and one or two of them gave little bows, and the others looked at them and they looked back at the others, but during that whole awkward comedy I don't remember any of them looking up at me. Finally the leader of the little troop cleared his throat.

"Consul Incitatus," he said. "We are very glad to have found you at last. Your presence is requested at the Capitol."

# CHAPTER TWELVE

Those soldiers hadn't a clue what to do with me, so they ignored me entirely, as though I were the consul's little dog that he had been taking for a walk. They didn't know what to do about the other horses, either, so they just let them come along too, even though some of them started getting excited and trotted on ahead. The whole procession became a bewildering muddle of soldiers and horses, with Incitatus and me strolling along in the middle.

I was very frightened now that I had come out of my daydream, but I had missed my chance to run. I could only hope that I remained as invisible as I appeared to be and that I might find another moment to escape later on. For a long time we walked through the dark streets, and if anyone was awake at that hour in Rome, they were very careful not to let the soldiers know it. There wasn't a lamp or a candle to be seen anywhere, and our only light was cast by the single guttering torch somewhere near the head of the procession.

But when we turned into the forum, there was suddenly light everywhere. And

people, gathered around the temples and the streets between them. They weren't in a big crowd but in small groups here and there, some standing, some sitting, some wrapped in blankets and sleeping.

We marched through them, and I saw eyes, one pair after another, turned toward us in weary bewilderment. And then someone spotted Incitatus, and the whole sleepy gathering suddenly came alive.

"The consul!" a woman shouted, and the news was taken up and bounced along the street.

"The consul is here!"

"Incitatus is found!"

"Consul Incitatus is on his way!"

I swear the horse understood. He arched his beautiful neck and lifted his feet high, dancing on his toes with all the raw energy of the racehorse in him and with all the haughty dignity of a Roman consul.

We were surrounded by light now as people closed in around us with their lamps and torches to get a better look. As we left the forum and began to climb the steep path up the Capitoline Hill, loose horses thundered through the patches of darkness beyond, kicking up their heels in excitement and tearing back to rejoin the throng.

Someone blew a long note on a horn. The soldiers, wide awake now and extremely proud of themselves, waved cheerfully at the onlookers. There were more people waiting at the top of the hill, and when we reached it, a cheer went up. With a sudden rush of exhilaration, I realized that something had changed. I wasn't sure why, but I knew that this city no longer felt like Little Boots's Rome.

# Chapter Thirteen

**N**ews ran ahead of us, so by the time Incitatus and I arrived at the doors  of the Capitol, the senators who had been dozing inside were awake and on their feet. When I saw them in their robes of office, I realized that this

was no place for me, and I chose that
moment to jump off.

I could easily have slipped away and vanished into the night, but I'd done a stupid
thing. I had wrapped the end of the chain
around my hand as we walked through
the streets of Rome, and
now I couldn't unwind it.

Incitatus didn't hesitate
for an instant. He strode
right in as though he owned
the place, and the pressure of
soldiers and onlookers behind us
pushed me along with him, still attached
to the golden chain. Behind us the doors
closed, shutting the loose horses and the
onlookers outside. The soldiers stayed

at the doors, acting as guards now, and Incitatus and I were on our own.

As though he knew exactly where he was going, he strode down the aisle that the standing senators had created. I managed to get my hand free of the chain, but it was too late now for me to get away. I glanced down at myself, suddenly aware that I had been wearing the same grubby tunic for a fortnight and that my feet, where they showed through my sandals, were as black as charcoal. But I didn't think anyone else noticed. I watched the faces as we passed. Every last eye was fixed upon the horse, and not a single one fell upon me. I was, to my relief, still invisible.

We were heading straight for the central point of the temple, where the statue of Jupiter, with Little Boots's head, always stood. But Jupiter/Little Boots was gone. In its place was a very small statue on a very tall pedestal. It wasn't grand, but it was Jupiter, and it bore no resemblance whatsoever to our corrupt emperor.

I was still gazing at it, trying to take in the significance of it, when our course was altered by a curve in the wall of senators, and after another few steps we came to a halt in front of a man in the fine robes of a consul. Behind him, surrounded by members of the praetorian guard, was an old man sitting in a heavy wooden chair. His chin had dropped onto his chest and he was fast asleep, but I recognized him all the same. Everyone in Rome knew that face. It was Little Boots's daft old uncle, Claudius.

# CHAPTER FOURTEEN

The other consul cleared his throat and spoke above the murmur of voices in the Capitol.

"Now that Consul Incitatus is here, we can continue with the proceedings at hand," he said.

The senators broke up their makeshift corridor and took seats in a semicircle around the other consul and Claudius, who was still asleep and gently snoring. I realized that Incitatus was standing with

his back to
them all, and as
unobtrusively
as I could,
I prodded
him in the
side until
he turned
around. This,
unfortunately,
brought me
to a position right beside the other consul, and he stared at me as if I was a bad
smell, which I quite possibly was. He
opened his mouth as if he was going to
speak to me, then thought better of it and
turned his attention to the assembly.

"It is the unanimous decision of the senators here gathered that, following the death of Gaius Caesar Augustus Germanicus, his uncle Claudius be immediately crowned the new Caesar."

It was true then, that rumor that had gone around. But I still couldn't believe my ears. Claudius? Emperor of Rome? It had to be some kind of joke.

To my right there was a mild kerfuffle as efforts were made to wake up the old man.

"W-w-w-what?" he stammered.

"I presume," the consul went on, "that this decision meets with the approval of Incitatus?"

Once again all heads turned in my

direction, but once again not one eye alighted on me. The horse stood proudly, soaking up all the attention but perfectly still. He made no gesture that could be taken as either approval or dissent. He didn't even blink.

I suddenly understood why it had been so important that Incitatus be found. The consent of both consuls was needed before a new emperor could be instated. Incitatus might be a horse, but he was still a consul, and without his approval Claudius could not officially be made Caesar.

Still the assembly waited. Something had to be done. I put out my hand, fingers closed, beneath Incitatus's muzzle, and thinking I had a treat for him, he dipped his head. Finding I had nothing, he lifted it again. It was all that was needed.

A cheer went through the assembly and Claudius was helped to his feet. The other consul put a purple robe around Claudius's shoulders and a laurel wreath on his head. There were more cheers, uproarious ones, and I heard them spread beyond the Capitol and into the square outside. I knew that soon the streets would be full of runners carrying the wonderful news across the city and gathering the masses to come and pay their respects to the new Caesar. I couldn't wait to see my family and tell them that I had been here in the Capitol to see old Claudius crowned.

But the proceedings here were not yet over. The other consul took center stage again and called for quiet. When at last he got it, he said, "I would like to suggest that, as Claudius Caesar's first act in office, he remove the travesty that is the shame of the Roman Empire and relieve

Incitatus of the consulship."

There was a burst of enthusiastic agree-
ment, and Claudius was led forward to
perform his first duty.

"Y-y-y-yes," he said. "I agree. N-n-nice
horse b-b-but not a c . . . a c . . . not a
consul. Not any l-l-longer, anyway."

Like hounds on a fallen stag, a pack of
senators descended upon poor Incitatus
and ripped off his purple blanket and his
beautiful head collar. The horse shrank
away from the pulling and dragging
hands, but there was nowhere for him to
go and he had to submit. Yet again I was
ignored, but when the horse had been
stripped of all his finery, someone did
think to push a piece of coarse rope into

my hand. I put it around Incitatus's neck and his nose and made a rough halter.

"Whom do you appoint in his place, Caesar?" said the remaining consul.

"Oh. Oh yes," said Claudius. "Wh-wh-who indeed?"

He looked

around in

bewilder-

ment, and

someone

in the

front

row of

seats

seized

the

opportunity to leap to his feet and stick his hand up.

"Yes," said Claudius, "y-y-you'll do, whatever your name is. T-t-temporarily. Until the n-n-next election."

There was another huge cheer. Someone tossed the horse's purple blanket at the newly appointed consul, and the entire assembly collapsed into fits of laughter. When order was finally restored, the new appointee, now dressed in proper consular garb, came forward and called for quiet.

"I have a suggestion for your second official pronouncement," he said. "I propose that you offer this horse, this sorry reminder of your nephew's reign, to the great god Jupiter. He has been offended by the madness of Little Boots, and Rome must make amends. What better way of doing that than to offer him the horse as a blood sacrifice?"

# CHAPTER FIFTEEN

N o!" I screamed. "No, no, no, no, no!"

But my cries were drowned out by the din of a hundred approving voices. Already senators were moving forward to take hold of Incitatus and bring him to the place of sacrifice, but there was another voice as well as mine clamoring to be heard above the mob.

"S-s-s-stop it! I c-c-command you to s-s-stop this n-n-now!"

Claudius was standing up and waving his arms around, but it was some time before he was noticed and order was called and the frenzied racket died down.

"I know why you have been so k-k-keen to ap-ap-appoint me your new emperor," said Claudius. "You all think you can push me around and m-m-make me do what you w-w-want. But this is what I w-w-want. This b-b-b-boy here has something to s-s-say. L-l-let him be heard."

And he turned and looked at me. And both the consuls looked as me as well, and all the senators.

I wasn't invisible any longer. The emperor himself had made me real: a human being with an opinion and a right to be heard. Tears erupted without warning and streamed down my face. I felt dirty and smelly and very, very small, but I had to speak up. It wasn't for me, you see. It was for Incitatus.

"Don't kill him," I said. "Please don't kill him. He didn't ask to be made into a consul. He couldn't help any of it. He's only a horse."

And he was. He knew, you see. I swear he did. Without his purple blanket and his fancy head collar he was just an old racehorse who had had his day. His head drooped as if he was ashamed. The proud spark had completely vanished from his eye.

And seeing him like that gave me an idea.

"Perhaps you should start your reign in a different way," I said, and I was so glad that it was old Claudius I was speaking to, because I could never have spoken to anyone else in authority that way. "Perhaps you should begin with an act of generosity instead of an act of violence."

There were murmurs of disapproval from the assembly, but Claudius held up his hand.

"G-g-go on," he said.

"I'm the son of a baker, sir," I said. "And your nephew, the emperor Gaius, he took all our horses away and left us with nothing to pull our carts. Give us this horse in return, sir. As a replacement for the ones he took."

There was more disapproval from the senators, but Claudius was grinning with delight.

"Yes," he said. "T-t-take him, boy, and let him deliver b-b-b-bread to the p-p-people of Rome. I can think of no better way for the consul Incitatus to end his days."

# CHAPTER SIXTEEN

**A**nd there he is now, as you can see. He has been pulling a bread cart for us ever since, day in and day out. And do you know what? He loves it—don't you, Incy? Never gets tired of it. Never puts a foot wrong. Willing and good-tempered whatever the hour and whatever the weather.

The thing is, all the dreadful things you heard about Little Boots are true. He was a monster; there's no two ways about it. I will never understand what made him do such terrible things, but I do understand one thing about him. I know why he loved this horse. There was never an animal like him—was there, Incy? See him there? Understands every word I say—don't you, boy?

But I can't stay here chatting all day. My bread's going stale. I'll tell you one last thing about this horse, though. If I was made emperor tomorrow, this lad would be made consul the day after that.

And the other one? I don't know who I'd pick. I've got a very clever little dog at home. People are strange creatures, in my opinion. You can never really trust them. They might start out well enough, but power always gets the better of them in the end. Mind you, it hasn't got the better of old Claudius yet, has it? Smart guy, that, pretending to be a fool and keeping on the right side of his nephew.

Not such a simpleton, though, is he? Best Caesar Rome ever had, if you ask me. Look, Incy agrees with me—don't you,

Incy? He knows what a narrow escape he had. Long live the emperor Claudius, that's what I say. And if Incy could speak, that's exactly what he'd say, too.

# Author's Note

Little Boots is based upon Caligula, who was emperor of Rome between AD 37 and 41. The background details in the story are based upon my research into his rule, but I have taken some liberties as well. He did have a favorite racehorse called Incitatus, and the horse did have its own living quarters and servants. But although Caligula threatened to make Incitatus a consul, he didn't actually do it.

It's also interesting to note that when Caligula died, the Roman senators were so eager to sweep away the memory of his authoritarian rule that they gathered in a different place than usual. Normally they met in the forum, but on this occasion they went to the top of one of the highest hills in Rome, to the Capitol.